The Upside-down Fish

by
Richard MacNeill

To the children

including the silent story
The Pondwater King

BUAIDH

This is the story
  of the upside-down fish,
    of the fish who started out
      upside-down.

Each new fish emerges
    from its egg right-side-up...

but this one did not.

From the day it was born,
it swam belly on top
and dorsal beneath.

"What is wrong with you?"
the others would say,
"You're always swimming
the wrong way."

"For you, down is down,
and for me, down is up."

"It's all well and good
to be silly and play,
but be serious now
and swim the right way."

"Ah, but this is much more fun!
It tickles to warm my belly in the sun
and my eyes look deep
to the things you shun."

"Now, don't be so rude."
came the older fish jeering,
"We know what is best
for fishies like you."

"I say fishies are
    free to choose."
the silly one
    told the rest.
"I am who I am,
    happy and true.
    All is good
and I have nothing
    to prove."

None in the school
    understood.
    They bubbled
with hurtful words.

But, the upside-down fish
would not be bothered
and always wore a smile.

"If it means that I'm me,
   if it means that I'm free,
      I'll gladly be strange to you."
and all its life, it was.

It befriended many creatures
               of the sea
   and grew to be old and wise,

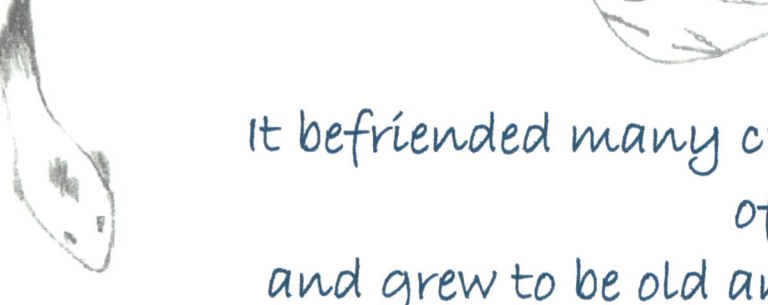

and breathing its final bubble,
it floated right-side-up
and still looked as cheerful as ever...

and among the young fishies
just born from their eggs,
one emerged swimming
belly on top
and dorsal beneath.